Minnie Mouse

Illustrated by Art Mawhinney

Published by
Louis Weber, C.E.O.
Publications International, Ltd.
7373 North Cicero Avenue
Lincolnwood, Illinois 60712

Lower Ground Floor, 59 Gloucester Place
London W1U 8JJ

Customer Service: 1-800-595-8484 or customer_service@pilbooks.com

www.pilbooks.com

p i kids is a trademark of Publications International, Ltd., and is registered in the United States.
Look and Find is a trademark of Publications International, Ltd., and is registered in the United States and Canada.

8 7 6 5 4 3 2 1

Manufactured in China.

ISBN: 978-1-4508-2544-3

 publications international, ltd.

Minnie is excited to have a relaxing day off. There's nothing more relaxing than sitting down with a good book. While Minnie browses the bookshelves for something to read, look for these friends who are also at the library:

Chip and Dale

Mickey

Donald

Daisy

Pluto

Uncle Scrooge

Goofy

Yummy! Minnie knows there's nothing like a sweet treat to help her relax. So she heads to the busy bakery, which is not very relaxing at all! While Minnie picks out a snack, look for each of these delicious desserts:

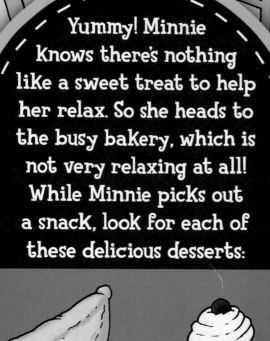

banana bread

red velvet cupcake

cinnamon bun

chocolate chip cookie

strawberry pie

carrot cake

donut

Some fresh flowers will brighten Minnie's day! So she goes to the greenhouse to buy some. But it's *so* busy. Gardening things and green thumbs are everywhere! Help Minnie pick a nice bouquet by finding these pretty plants:

cactus

venus flytrap

lemon tree

daisy

peanut plant

bonsai tree

watermelon plant

wreath made of roses

tomato plant

Oh, dear!
Minnie's in the middle
of a busy parking lot, and
her car has a flat tire!
Luckily, she knows how to
fix it all by herself. While
Minnie works on her car,
look for these other types of
transportation all around her:

pogo
stick

kite

scooter

roller skates

skateboard

bicycle

Now that her hands are all dirty from changing her tire, Minnie decides to go get a manicure. The beauty salon's as busy as can be. While Minnie soaks her tired hands, look for these beauty-related things:

shaving cream

hair trimmer

cucumber slices

nail clippers

shampoo

hair dryer

PET SHOW

Minnie is on her way home, ready to relax, when she passes the Blue Ribbon Pet Show. Always a good friend, she stops to cheer for Pluto and Mickey. While Minnie roots for her pals, look for these other animals who want to win:

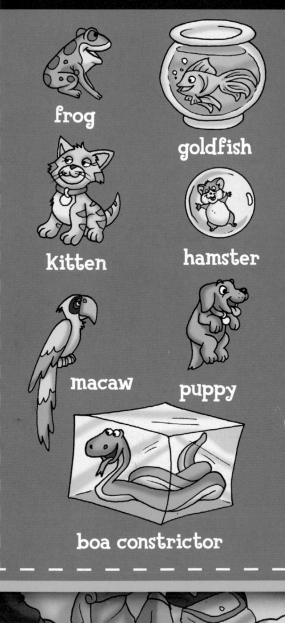

frog

goldfish

kitten

hamster

macaw

puppy

boa constrictor

To celebrate Pluto's blue ribbon, Minnie and Mickey are taking him for a walk in the park. But it's not a very relaxing way to end the day. Look for these crazy things that are going on:

At last, Minnie's busy day is done and it's time to relax. But look! Minnie is too tired to enjoy her book or flowers or treat. She has fallen right to sleep! While Minnie snoozes, search for these things she picked up during the day:

library book

a bouquet

nail polish

jack for her car

pluto's blue ribbon

cupcake

Go back to the library and find these storybook characters hidden around the scene:

- Humpty Dumpty
- Little Red Riding Hood
- Mother Goose
- Big Bad Wolf
- Rumpelstiltskin
- Emperor wearing new clothes
- Three Little Pigs

Get back in line at the bakery and look for these baking ingredients:

- milk
- eggs
- icing
- chocolate chips
- °our
- sugar
- banana

Tiptoe through the tulips until you get to the greenhouse. Then search for these things that might help your garden grow:

- watering can
- °owerpot
- packet of seeds
- hoe
- bag of fertilizer
- hose

Pull back into the parking lot and look for these silly vehicles:

- dogsled
- clown car
- Mickey Mouse's car
- ice-cream cart
- Scrooge's fancy car
- balloon cart
- Donald's car in a fender bender

Slip back into the beauty salon and seek out these stylish services:

- shampoo
- haircut
- massage
- pedicure
- shave
- mud mask

Scamper, soar, swim, or slither back to the Blue Ribbon Pet Show and look for these pets you don't see every day:

fox

timber wolf

stingray

komodo dragon

dodo

beaver

Stroll back through the park and spot these more normal outdoor items:

soccer ball

golf club

bread for feeding ducks

...ing ...isc

picnic basket

foot bag

Quietly go back to Minnie's house to find 12 matching pairs of plants: